Before reading

Look at the book cover together
Ask, "What do you think will

To build independen ... cluded
at the start of th ... turn
back to pag ... ain with
the child.

During read

Offer plenty of supp ... e as the child reads the story.
Listen carefully and re ... to events in the text.

When a **Key Word** is used for the first time, it is also shown at the bottom of the page. If the child hesitates over a word, point to the **New Key Words** box and practise reading it together. If the word is phonically decodable, you can sound out the letters and blend the sounds to read the word ("d-o-g, dog"). Praise the child for their effort, then return to the story.

Pause every few pages and ask questions to check the child's understanding of what they have read. If they begin to lose concentration, stop reading and save the page for later.

Celebrate the child's achievement and come back to the story the next day.

After reading

After reading this book, ask, "Did you enjoy the story? What did you like about it?" Encourage the child to share their opinions.

Use the comprehension questions on page 54 to check the child's understanding and recall of the text.

Ladybird

Series Consultant: Professor David Waugh
With thanks to Kulwinder Maude

LADYBIRD BOOKS

UK | USA | Canada | Ireland | Australia
India | New Zealand | South Africa

Ladybird Books is part of the Penguin Random House group of companies
whose addresses can be found at global.penguinrandomhouse.com.
www.penguin.co.uk www.puffin.co.uk www.ladybird.co.uk

Penguin Random House UK

Original edition of Key Words with Peter and Jane first published by Ladybird Books Ltd 1964
Series updated 2023
This book first published 2023
001

With thanks to Liz Pemberton for her contributions in advising on the illustrations
With thanks to Inclusive Minds for connecting us with their Inclusion Ambassador network,
and in particular thanks to Guntaas Kaur Chugh for her input on the illustrations

Printed in China

The authorized representative in the EEA is Penguin Random House Ireland,
Morrison Chambers, 32 Nassau Street, Dublin D02 YH68

A CIP catalogue record for this book is available from the British Library

ISBN: 978-0-241-51089-6

All correspondence to:
Ladybird Books
Penguin Random House Children's
One Embassy Gardens, 8 Viaduct Gardens, London SW11 7BW

FSC www.fsc.org MIX Paper from responsible sources FSC® C018179

Key Words

with Peter and Jane

6b

Sun, sea and sand

Based on the original

Key Words with Peter and Jane

reading scheme and research by William Murray

Original edition written by William Murray

This edition written by Zoë Clarke

Illustrated by Gustavo Mazali

A big boat was sailing on the water with Peter and Jane on board.

"This is fun! The boat is jumping in and out of the sea," Peter said.

But Jane started to feel sick. She had to hang on to the rail.

Tess barked at the water.

New Key Words

out of sea said but had

After all the jumping in and out of the sea, the boat was near the dock.

"This holiday will be fun," Dad said.

Mum said, "Look! There are our friends!"

Yaz and Mike had come to meet them.

New Key Words

after all holiday our them

They walked from the dock to the village.

Jane liked the Sun, Swim and Sea shop.

"Look at all the fish!" Peter said. "I like them."

Tess liked the ice cream.

New Key Words

walk from village sun

swim ice cream

Yaz and Mike had a big house near the sea.

"Where are the boys?" said Mum.

"Krish and Rohan are out in our little boat," Yaz said.

Peter and Jane liked Krish and Rohan.

New Key Words

house where

Jane looked out to sea.

“I can see Krish and Rohan,” she said. “Can we walk down to the sea?”

Mum said, “Yes, off you go.”

New Key Words

Peter and Jane walked from the house to where Rohan and Krish's boat was.

"Can you see us?" Peter and Jane said.

Krish and Rohan looked pleased to see them.

New Key Words

After Rohan and Krish had sailed into the boat house, they all walked up to the big house.

“Dad and Mum will like sitting here in the sun,” said Peter.

“But where are they?” Krish said.

New Key Words

but

"There they are!" said Jane.
They had tents.

"You can all sleep out here," Mike said.

"But you have to help us make the tents," Mum said.

New Key Words

us make

"This bit must go here,"
Krish said. "But which bit goes here?"

"Where can this thing fit?"
Jane said.

Rohan had all the string.
"Where do I put this string?"
he said.

"Have you all read this?"
Peter said.

New Key Words

must which read

They all read it, and, after a bit of help, they put up all the tents.

"I can see the sea from our tent," Peter said.

"The tents are like holiday houses," Jane said. "Tess, you can keep the animals out of our holiday house."

New Key Words

keep

"Can we go and get ice creams, please?" Peter said.

Rohan and Krish walked with them to the village.

They walked into the Sun, Swim and Sea shop.

"Look at all the flags," Jane said. "Our holiday house must have one."

New Key Words

After going to the shop,
they all had an ice cream.
Peter read out the list of
ice creams.

"Which ice cream will you
have?" Jane said.

"A green ice cream, please,"
Peter said.

New Key Words

They all walked from the village to the big house.

At the house, Jane and Krish had fun hanging the flag from the tent.

Peter and Rohan had books to read. They sat in the sun with Tess.

New Key Words

After tea, they walked down to the sea.

“We can have a swim,” Rohan said.

They pulled out some swim things.

“I can swim to the boat house,” Jane said.

“I can swim to the dock,” said Peter.

New Key Words

"Aunt Liz and Uncle Jack!" yelled Jane.

They had come for a holiday with them all.

Tess jumped in and out of the sea near them.

New Key Words

aunt uncle

After the swim, the children sat near the tents. Tess sat with them.

"This will be fun!" Uncle Jack said. He and Aunt Liz put up a red tent for them.

Peter and Jane had things to read. Krish and Rohan played a game.

New Key Words

After dark, Peter and Jane slept. But after a bit, the wind started rushing.

"The tent flaps keep swinging!" Peter said.

Jane jumped up. "We must shut them," she said.

New Key Words

But Peter was wet. There was water in the tent.

Krish and Rohan jumped out of the tent. “We are all wet!” they said.

“Our tent is all wet!” said Uncle Jack.

New Key Words

“Where can we go?” Jane said.

Krish said, “We can all run to our house and sleep there.”

“Let’s go!” said Aunt Liz.

New Key Words

After a good sleep, they all walked to the sea. The sun was out!

Aunt Liz and Uncle Jack walked to where the sea had washed up shells.

"Some of the rocks have things in them," Aunt Liz said.

Peter said, "Where can I get a rock like that?"

New Key Words

"We must make a list of all the things we see near the sea on our holiday," said Jane.

"Look at the water," said Uncle Jack. "Where do the fish come from?"

"The sea," said Jane.

She walked on the rocks and looked at the fish swimming in the water. She picked up a rock near her.

New Key Words

"The sea is rushing in, Jane," said Aunt Liz. "Can you walk to us?"

Uncle Jack said, "We must walk on the rocks from here. Keep going, Jane! Keep going!"

"You can make it to us!" Peter said.

Jane jumped.

"Yes, I can make it," she said.

New Key Words

They walked to the fish-and-chip van in the village.

"But there are no fish left for us," Uncle Jack said.

They all had chips.

New Key Words

"Where is that rock?" Peter said. "Which bag is it in?"

Jane had the rock in her bag, but the rock had cracked.

Jane had a fish after all!

New Key Words

Questions

Answer these questions about the story.

1 Why does Jane feel sick on the boat?

2 What are the children's "holiday houses"?

3 What does Jane get at the Sun, Swim and Sea shop?

4 Why do the children, Aunt Liz and Uncle Jack sleep in Krish and Rohan's house?

5 What do Peter and Jane see in the rock at the end of the story?